HUNGRY SHARK®

SHARK
OUT OF
WATER!

SHARK
OUT OF
WATER!

By Ace Landers

Book 1

Featuring the stars of

SCHOLASTIC INC.

Special thanks to our chums at Ubisoft and Future Games of London, and a jaw-some thanks to Sam Fry, Valentina Marchetti, Caroline Lamache, Anthony Marcantonio, Lena Barendt, Thomas Veyrat, James Varma, and Giorgia La Rocca.

The publisher does not have any control over and does not assume any responsibility for author or third-party websites or their content.

This book is a work of fiction. Names, characters, places, and incidents are either the product of the author's imagination or are used fictitiously, and any resemblance to actual persons, living or dead, business establishments, events, or locales is entirely coincidental.

ISBN: 978-1-338-56871-4

10 9 8 7 6 5 4 3 2 1   20 21 22 23 24

Printed in the U.S.A. 40
First edition 2020

Book design by Mercedes Padró

ONE
The Best Things Take Time

Tammy's watch was broken. It *had* to be.

"It's not three-twenty," Tammy muttered, adjusting the knob on her watch. "It can't be."

She was sitting atop a desk in science class. Aside from Tammy, the only other person in the room was her best friend, Kyle, who sat behind her. Whereas Tammy was fixated on the time, Kyle was drawing in a sketchbook.

Kyle loved to draw, but when people asked him what he liked to illustrate, he'd shrug and say, "Interesting things," as if that explained everything. (It never did.)

It appeared, however, that today's Interesting Thing was a logo for the Marine Science Club. Admittedly, Kyle didn't care much for marine science, but Tammy did. And if something mattered to Tammy, then it mattered to Kyle. (Mostly, anyway.)

"The flyer definitely said three, right? Not three-thirty?" Tammy asked hopefully.

Kyle shook his head.

"The best things take time," he replied. "Maybe no one is interested in joining Marine Science Club *now*, but this time next month, they'll be clamoring outside just to get in. There'll be so many kids we'll have to move weekly meetings to the auditorium. We'll be the coolest club at school."

Tammy smiled at her friend. "I hope so," she replied, then lowered her voice. "Marine science is just so *cool*."

Kyle smiled back. He wanted to cheer up Tammy. "Hey, take a peek at the logo I've been drawing. Maybe this'll convince some kids to join."

Tammy looked down at Kyle's sketchbook. He had hand-lettered the words MARINE SCIENCE CLUB in neat curved letters. Underneath those words he had drawn a shark that looked as if it were about to jump off the page. It had one big eye, a pointed fin, and lots of razor-sharp teeth.

"Kyle!" Tammy said. "Where was this two days ago?"

"What'd I say? The best things take time. You can't rush *art*!" Kyle replied.

The two friends laughed. Kyle could always make Tammy laugh. He could make anyone laugh, actually. That was what Tammy admired most about him.

Just then, there was a loud voice at the door. Tammy jumped. She was so invested in their conversation that she had completely forgotten they were still at school—even if it *was* a Friday afternoon.

"Oh *no!*" the voice hollered. It was coming from a black-haired boy who rushed into the room. He was short and scrawny, and he was wearing a black T-shirt with a rock band logo on it. "Is the meeting already over? Did I miss the MSC?"

"The Music Sound Club meets in Ms. Ricci's room," Tammy replied. "My friend Kyle and I are just about to leave anyway. We can walk over with you if you'd like."

The boy looked very confused. "Music Sound Club?" he repeated. "No, not *that* MSC. The Marine Science Club! Fish, ocean, yeah? That's here, right?"

Tammy's eyes widened. She exchanged a quick glance with Kyle, as if to say, *Is this really happening?*

"Oh! Yes!" Tammy nearly shouted. "You're looking right at it! And if you're interested, you're our third official member. What's your name?"

The kid fist-pumped excitedly in the air. "My name's Alexander de la Cruz. But everyone calls me Alex. I just moved here. There wasn't a Marine Science Club at my old school, but I think it's an awesome idea. The best idea, actually. I really wish I'd thought of it first, but I'm glad I didn't have to. Hey! Is that a shark?"

Alex spoke very quickly, but he paused and pointed to Kyle's drawing.

"No, that's my grandfather," Kyle said very seriously. Then he laughed. "I'm just kidding. Of course, it's a shark!"

"I was about to say . . . that sounded *fishy*," Alex replied, not missing a beat. Tammy chuckled. "What kind of shark is it?"

"It's a porbeagle," Kyle replied. "I was looking up cool sharks to draw and this one popped up. It's a medium-sized shark mostly found in the Atlantic Ocean, and its name is a combo of 'porpoise' and 'beagle,' because it kind of looks like a porpoise and kind of hunts like a beagle."

"Isn't that just a theory, though?" Alex said, as quickly as before. "I've read that 'porbeagle' is a combination of the Cornish word for harbor— *porth*—and *bugel*, which means shepherd."

"Possibly. But then wouldn't that just be a theory too?" Kyle replied, smiling.

"My dad thinks this necklace is from a porbeagle shark, but I'm not convinced," said Alex, taking a shark-tooth necklace on a chain out from underneath his T-shirt. "But the tooth is not as pointy as a porbeagle's tooth, see? And it's longer. It's my good luck charm. I picked it up on the beach when I first moved here a few weeks ago, and I'd really like to figure out what kind of shark it's from."

Tammy's head zoomed back and forth between Alex and Kyle. She always knew that Kyle did a *lot* of research on his Interesting Things, but where had this new kid been hiding? He knew even more about sharks than she did, and she'd studied marine animals with her grandfather last summer in Japan!

"Okay, nerds." Tammy smiled affectionately. "As much as I love this chitchat, we're off-topic. Now that we're a group of three, we can be an official organization represented by the school. So first things first, we have to vote on a president, and then I can get this organization application over to Principal Sutker."

"Well, I think that answer's obvious," Kyle said, "but Waverly Middle School *is* a democracy, so let's vote. Who thinks Tammy Aiko, founder of this club, should be president?"

Kyle and Alex both raised their hands high.

"Thanks, guys. And who wants to be my VP?" Tammy asked.

"You should," Kyle said, gesturing to Alex.

Alex nodded, accepting his role dutifully.

"And do you want a position, Kyle? Maybe secretary? Or treasurer?"

Kyle thought for a moment. "Nah," he said, shaking his head. "I'm here to support you, Tammy. And, uh, all of marine science!"

Tammy shot him a curious look, but then decided against saying anything. "Well, it looks like Marine Science Club is a go!" she announced, finishing up the organization paperwork.

"I feel like we need a secret handshake or something," Kyle said.

"How about we pump our fists together and say, '*Science!*'?" Alex suggested. Then he demonstrated the motion.

"Hmm. Maybe something a little . . . cooler," Tammy replied. She was thinking about the rest of the school joining in. She couldn't really imagine kids like Leo McCormack chanting "Science."

"The best things take time," Tammy said, repeating her friend's advice. "A handshake will come. Besides, it's getting late. Let's all meet this weekend at the beach to do some hands-on marine science stuff and really get things going. Alex, here's my phone. Text yourself so that you get my number, and I'll save yours."

Tammy took her phone out of her back pocket and handed it to Alex, who did as instructed. Then, she saved his contact information in her phone as Alex 🦈🦈, making sure to put not one but *two* emojis, because that was what she did for all her favorite people.

TWO
Shark Time

When Tammy got home, she made a list of all the things she could do to make Marine Science Club cool.

- Post pretty pics of marine science stuff to social media.
- Host a school-wide field trip.
- Plan an ice cream party.

The school-wide field trip and ice cream party were good ideas. But MSC wasn't there yet. If Tammy wanted to make Marine Science Club cool, she'd have to start small.

"First step: Take some pretty pictures," Tammy muttered to herself. "I think we can handle that."

•

On Saturday morning, Tammy made a group chat for the members of the Marine Science Club.

Tammy

MSC meeting today. Tiburon Beach boardwalk?

Kyle 🍄🍄

👍

Alex 🦈🦈

Sounds great!!!

Perfect! Let's meet at Tasha's Italian Ice at noon.

Alex 🐬🐬

I can't wait! C you all soon!!! 😌

Waverly Middle School students were lucky because Tiburon Beach was so close. It was about two miles away from the school, which was the perfect distance for kids' parents to drive them after class.

Tammy loved it at the beach. There was the boardwalk filled with fair rides and games. When Tammy was six, she won a stuffed seal at the water blaster race game, and she still slept with it on her bed. The boardwalk had everything, from Tasha's Italian Ice to fancy seafood restaurants to T-shirt shops and sunscreen stands. At the end of the boardwalk was a pier that stretched out into the ocean. Locals liked to fish there. Tammy used to visit a lot with her grandfather when she was younger. He'd point out interesting facts about the waves, and she'd smile and listen intently because it was her favorite place in the world.

But today, Tammy didn't just want to traverse the boardwalk or the pier. She wanted to meet there, sure, but then do something else. Go on an adventure. Make the Marine Science Club *cool*.

Tammy dressed in her usual beach attire, which was a pair of denim shorts, a blue T-shirt, and a bathing suit underneath. She swept her long dark hair up into a ponytail and tied a purple ribbon around it. The ribbon was a gift from her grandfather—he'd proudly told her that it was biodegradable, meaning if it got lost, it wouldn't contribute to pollution.

Then Tammy's mom drove her to the MSC meeting point. Tammy knew Kyle was usually late, but she was surprised to see that Alex was already waiting for her.

"My parents own the new pizza spot right next to Tasha's," Alex said, noting Tammy's puzzled look. "That's why we moved here, actually. They make the best pizza ever. My mom thinks it's her crust that makes it extra delicious, but I think it's my grandma's secret sauce."

Tammy smiled.

"That's amazing," she said. "I love pizza. Maybe we can go there when the meeting is over."

"Yeah, I'm sure my parents would love that! Hey, while we wait for Kyle, why don't we grab some Italian ice now?" Alex suggested.

Tammy agreed. She could always go for some Italian ice! She bought two scoops of cherry Italian ice (one for Alex, one for her), and they sat on one of the benches outside and dug in.

"So how are you liking your new house? Waverly Middle?" Tammy asked. "I've lived here my whole life, so I don't really know anything different."

"I like it so far," Alex said. "But it's been kind of hard to make friends. I feel like everyone's so obsessed over what's cool and what's trendy. You've got to have the latest phone, the newest computer, stuff like that. And I like being trendy too, but it's a little overwhelming."

"Well, it looks like you found the *least* trendy club out there," Tammy said, laughing. "For now, anyway. But I'm glad you did."

"Me too," replied Alex. "And I wouldn't say that. Just you wait! All good things—"

". . . take time," Tammy said, finishing Alex's sentence. Then she turned around. Someone had finished the sentence with her—Kyle!

"Took ya long enough," Tammy said, sweeping Kyle into a big hug. "All right. Now we're ready to go for an adventure. Time for Marine Science Club meeting number two!"

Alex fist-pumped the air and yelled, *"Science!"* Then he smiled at the two of them.

"One day you're going to like it," he said.

"Don't hold your breath," Tammy joked back. Then she was all business. "Now that we're all here, it's important we set Marine Science Club out from the crowd by doing something *really fun*. And taking photos. So I was thinking, let's head out to... Tiburon Cove."

"Tiburon Cove?" Alex repeated. "What's that?"

"You can't be serious," said Kyle at the same time. "Tammy, *no one* goes to Tiburon Cove. It's nicknamed Stinkerton Cove, remember? It stinks. Bad. Like rotten eggs." Kyle pinched his nose with his fingers.

"Well, it might *smell* bad, but it's also really beautiful down there," Tammy replied. "We can snap some pics of the tide pools and post them to our new social media accounts, maybe even submit them to the school paper. People need to know about MSC. We need to up our *awareness.*" When she said that, Tammy channeled her cousin Alison, who was a freshman at Waverly College studying marketing.

Before Alex or Kyle could say anything else, Tammy started strutting toward the cove. And then Alex and Kyle followed, because that was what best friends did.

•

When the three friends arrived at Tiburon Cove, Tammy had to admit that Kyle was right. It *stunk* down there. But she tried not to let it get to her.

"Hey, what's that?" Kyle asked, and pointed to a little ripple inside a tide pool.

Tammy whipped her head over. Inside the tide pool was a tiny hermit crab easing into the wet mud.

"That's a hermit crab," explained Alex.

"Fun fact: Hermit crabs are not true crabs. They are actually more like lobsters."

Kyle opened up the sketchbook he'd been carrying. As he did, Tammy smiled at him. She realized that Kyle had found his daily Interesting Thing.

And if the hermit crab was interesting to Kyle, Tammy reasoned, then it might just be interesting to the Waverly Middle School student body too. She took out her phone and angled the lens just right. Then she snapped a photo of the crab.

"This is going to make an *excellent* first post," Tammy said, admiring the hermit crab both in real life and in the pixels on her phone. She was playing with the brightness settings of the photo when Alex tapped her on the shoulder.

"I didn't know dolphins get close to Tiburon Beach," he said, pointing to a spot in the not-so-distant horizon. It looked like a glimmer among the growing waves at first, but then it popped up again. It was right outside of the cave they were standing in.

Kyle stopped sketching to take a look. "Whoa, I can see their pointy back things peeking out of the water."

"Pointy back things? I think you mean dorsal fins. That's pretty cool," Tammy said.

A pod of dolphins, after all, was way cooler than a tiny hermit crab. Hermit crabs were interesting, but dolphins were material for the front page of the Waverly school newspaper. Tammy took out a pair of binoculars from her backpack. She needed to inspect the dolphins even more closely.

Tammy adjusted her binoculars and zoomed in. Sure enough, a gray fin broke the surface, followed by a second and a third. The animals were moving in rhythm. But they didn't look like dolphins . . .

"Guys," said Tammy slowly. "Those are sharks! Three different sharks!"

She passed her binoculars to Alex and Kyle. They shared the binoculars by each taking one eyepiece.

"Whoa," Kyle said.

"That's amazing," Alex added.

Tammy smiled to herself. It *was* amazing. One shark by itself would have been amazing, but *three* sharks? Even more amazing. And what were the odds?

Tammy *had* to get a photo of the sharks for the school paper. She *had* to. Nothing would make Marine Science Club cooler.

Tammy could just imagine the headline now: SPOT SHARKS WITH THE MARINE SCIENCE CLUB! Tammy's face pasted right in, next to those of Alex and Kyle. "We weren't really expecting anything when we went to Tiburon Cove . . ." Tammy's quote would start off. Then they'd interview the hundreds of other members who had joined MSC, because when you were a club that spotted sharks, you got hundreds of members. You got to be the coolest club at school.

Coolest club at school. Tammy could almost taste it.

"Come on," she told her friends, urging them to get closer. "It's shark time, baby."

THREE
Keep Swimming, Keep Chomping

Of course, that was how Tammy, Kyle, and Alex found the sharks.

But how did the sharks find the humans?

Earlier that day, Hammerhead was swimming to her special place, an old sunken ship that used to belong to a pirate. Aside from Hammerhead's best friends, Porbeagle and Mako, most other sharks didn't care for the old sunken ship, but Hammerhead loved it.

She liked to swim around and stick her head through the skeletons with funny hats and poke around little sticks that the humans must have used as peg legs.

Hammerhead had a collection of human things. Of course, not everyone was happy about that. Hammerhead had been swimming around one day with an eye patch when she ran into Tiger Shark. Tiger Shark was Hammerhead's friend, but Tiger Shark still liked to tease her.

Whatcha got there, Hams? Tiger seemed to say.

None of your sharkswax! Hammerhead motioned back.

Tiger didn't take no for an answer. He kept lightly bumping into Hammerhead, trying to get Hammerhead to reveal what was curled up in her fin. Finally, Hammerhead showed him.

Tiger seemed to laugh. Tiger was one of the toughest sharks in the sea. He could flatten out a whole ecosystem with one swipe of his tail. And as much as Hammerhead hated to admit it . . . Tiger was the *coolest* shark she knew.

Give it to me! Tiger all but hissed, motioning for Hammerhead to hand the eye patch over.

No. Hammerhead shook her head.

Tiger didn't like that.

Hammerhead tried to stand her ground again, but unfortunately, once Tiger decided he wanted something, he got it.

Tiger mustered all his might and body-slammed Hammerhead. Although Hammerhead tried to keep the eye patch in her fin, it was no use. The patch slipped out of her hold and into the deep ocean below. Then Tiger made a mad dash for it.

Hammerhead tried going after it too, but she was too late. Tiger was *fast*. In just a few moments, the hulking Tiger Shark had the eye patch wrapped firmly around his own eye. He cast a toothy smile at Hammerhead, as if to say, *Smell ya later*. Then he was gone—and so was Hammerhead's precious eye patch.

The memory made Hammerhead's eyes prickle. She had really wanted that eye patch. She was planning something very important.

You see, Hammerhead was *fascinated* with terrestrial life. Even if the other sharks weren't, or made fun of her for it or said she wasn't *cool*, Hammerhead just wanted to learn more about land-dwelling creatures. Breathe out of the water? That seemed like a thing only a superhero could do.

Thankfully, today, Hammerhead was pleased. Aboard the pirate ship, she had found a new oddity to add to her collection—a beautiful glass bowl.

The bowl was exactly what Hammerhead needed for her newest task: a land suit!

With a land suit, she could go where no shark had gone before (and lived to tell the tale) . . . the *land*.

Thus far, Hammerhead had collected an eggbeater, a trumpet, a tire, and a snorkel mask. That snorkel mask was what gave her the idea to build the land suit in the first place, actually. She just needed a bowl that would fit over her head and hold enough water for her to breathe. And now she had the perfect one!

Hammerhead stopped to admire her bowl again and try it on. She also wanted to make sure none of the other sharks were spying on her. If Tiger caught her, she'd never hear the end of it. But if Hammerhead's invention worked, she knew that Tiger would be the first in line to try it out.

As she slipped on the bowl, Hammerhead heard it click into place. The silence of the ocean became even quieter.

Now it was time for step two: walking practice. If Hammerhead was ever going to travel above the water, she needed to know how to walk, because swimming on land—well, it just doesn't work. She'd seen lots of other animals try, like those whales who kept getting stuck on the beach and the fish who got caught (they'd *blub, blub, blub* and never *once* got to walk for real). She didn't want to suffer the embarrassment of having humans roll her back into the water. She knew Tiger would probably sell tickets to that kind of event!

Carefully, Hammerhead placed her tail on the ocean floor. Using all her concentration, she slowly straightened her back until she stood up. A school of young fish swam around the corner and stared at her. Hammerhead knew she must have looked silly to them, but she didn't care. They were fish. If they laughed at her, she'd just eat them. Problem solved.

When she was steady on her fins, Hammerhead took her first step. It worked! Then a second . . . then a third . . . until she was walking toward her sunken pirate ship.

Of course her walking wasn't the *best* walking in the world, but Hammerhead decided that since she was a shark, after all, it might be good enough.

She had just wobbled forward when she heard a dull thumping noise coming from behind. Hammerhead froze. She knew what that dull thumping noise meant.

It meant a *shark*.

Was it Tiger? Hammerhead closed her eyes. She wanted to spend the next second of not knowing for sure in total bliss. Then she opened them, one by one. There was a tail—

Phew. Hammerhead blew a bubble as a

sign of relief. The shark nearing her was half swimming, half bouncing with the excitement of a giant puppy dog. Hammerhead had learned all about "puppy dogs" from a laminated magazine that she had found underwater. Puppy dogs, the article explained, were man's—and woman's—best friend. And although this wasn't some kind of aquatic puppy dog, it *was* Porbeagle.

Porbeagle was Hammerhead's best friend. Albeit her *clumsy* best friend.

CRASH! Porbeagle pounced directly on Hammerhead and knocked her down. Hammerhead's mask flew off her head. She watched as the key part of her land suit flipped through the water in slow motion, then shattered against the ocean floor.

Hammerhead tried to stop it, but it was

too late. The hermit crabs crawled from their hiding places and used the broken pieces as new homes. Hammerhead's perfect helmet, her beautiful glass bowl, was gone.

Porbeagle, of course, didn't notice anything except for the fact that he had found his best friend. He gave Hammerhead a big, slobbery lick with his tongue. It sounded kind of like this: *Slurrrrrp!*

Hammerhead pushed Porbeagle to the side and shook herself off. She wanted to be mad at Porbeagle, but gazing at her friend's puppy-dog eyes, she knew she could never stay angry for long. Hammerhead knew that Porbeagle, unlike Tiger, meant no harm.

Porbeagle noticed the hermit crabs scurry to their new glass homes and swam over to inspect them. He sniffed them first, then picked one up in his mouth and spit it out. *Hermit crabs do not taste good*, Porbeagle decided. They were too crunchy.

Just as Porbeagle thought the hermit crab would scurry off, it turned around and snapped at his nose with its claw. *Ouch!* Porbeagle thought. *That hurt!* He then made a very important observation. *Hermit crabs are crunchy, but they are also claw-y.*

Porbeagle decided he should not eat hermit crabs unless he was really, really hungry.

Then the playful shark turned and looked for his friend, but Hammerhead had already retreated into the sunken ship. Porbeagle swam after her through the hole in the side of the boat.

Porbeagle loved the inside of Hammerhead's ship. It was filled with all her weird inventions. Porbeagle didn't know why Hammerhead loved to build things so much, especially when there was tons of food in the ocean to eat! But he knew that all sharks were different.

Hammerhead floated in front of a map that hung on the wall. It showed the local ocean floor, but Hammerhead had circled all of the spots where she found cool treasures from the surface. There were a lot of circles near a place called Tiburon Cove.

Hammerhead pointed to the cove on the map, but Porbeagle wasn't paying attention. He had just spotted a bright pink fish trying to sneak by them. Quickly, Porbeagle snapped it up, and although it was very delicious, the chewy fish gave out a loud *"squeak-er! squeak-er!"* with every bite.

Hammerhead hated that noise. She swam over and pulled the fish out of Porbeagle's mouth. She shook her head at Porbeagle and showed him that the fish was not a fish, but instead one of the treasures from above the water that she had found.

She squeezed the fish in her fin, and the fish made the same squeaking sound. Porbeagle did an eager flip, as if this were the beginning of a game.

But Hammerhead was in no mood to play. She was on a mission! She needed to find another bowl for her invention. The first bowl had been half buried in the sea floor near Tiburon Cove. Maybe she could find another bowl there?

Porbeagle kept snapping at the fake fish, so Hammerhead threw it as far as she could.

Unfortunately (or rather fortunately, depending on whose side you take), Porbeagle *was* in the mood to play, so he raced after the fish squeaker and returned a few seconds later with the pink fish victoriously clamped in his mouth.

Hammerhead had way more important things to do than play with Porbeagle. And she could tell that this squeaker fish needed to disappear quickly. So Hammerhead took the fish outside and buried it deep in the sand while Porbeagle watched, very confused.

When Hammerhead was done, she shrugged at Porbeagle as if to say, *I don't know where that pink fish went, but it's gone for good now.*

But Porbeagle knew that wasn't true! He dove into the dirt, spinning like a power drill, and found the squeaker in no time.

Filthy and covered with mud, Porbeagle swam over to Hammerhead and dropped the bright fish in front of her. Then he bounced around, ready to play some more.

Hmm, thought Hammerhead, smiling widely and flashing her sharp teeth. She suddenly had a plan for how to find another bowl. And she was sure that Porbeagle would *dig* it.

FOUR
Mako-ing New Friends

That plan was Tiburon Cove.

Hammerhead was excited to venture back there. She hoped that maybe, for shark's sake, there would be another perfect glass bowl. Maybe one even *better* than the last. If she was really, really lucky, maybe there would even be a whole land suit tailored to her!

Hammerhead would quickly travel two swishes, but then turn around to see that

Porbeagle was chasing either a jellyfish or an eel. It was a good thing that Hammerhead had brought the bright fish squeaker to get her friend's attention. Otherwise, she wasn't sure how they would make it to Tiburon Cove.

The idea for the land suit had come when Hammerhead spotted a group of deep sea divers one day. The humans wore masks to help them breathe air underwater as they explored the ocean. But when Hammerhead swam over to inspect how their masks worked, the divers were not as excited to see her as they were to see the other fish in the sea.

The divers saw Hammerhead and swam away faster than a sailfish in a riptide! Hammerhead was pretty sure she even heard them scream in horror, but when she looked around, she couldn't see anything scary in the ocean. Humans were very weird like that. Hammerhead was only trying to be friendly!

When Hammerhead and Porbeagle had almost reached the cove, Porbeagle stopped and raised his ear. He heard the strangest noise. Hammerhead stopped too, because even *she* heard the noise. It sounded like the entire ocean was splashing. They could feel the ripples echoing everywhere.

Suddenly, Hammerhead and Porbeagle were surrounded by panicked schools of colorful fish that fluttered past them in a wake of a thousand tiny waves. Hammerhead covered her eyes—she was always getting poked in the eyes. Porbeagle, on the other hand, took a few yummy bites. After all, it was not every day that your dinner jumped right into your mouth.

In a flash, the fish were gone and a fast-moving shadow appeared. Hammerhead immediately knew who it was: Mako.

●

Great, thought Hammerhead. *First Porbeagle, now Mako!* She loved her friends, but it was as if the ocean didn't want her to finish building her land suit.

Mako was one of Hammerhead's dearest friends, but he was . . . well, *loud*. When Mako was a baby shark, he found a giant metal box at the bottom of the sea. Like any normal shark, Mako was curious about it. The side of the box had strange writing on it that looked like this: H-O-T C-H-O-C-O-L-A-T-E.

Mako couldn't read, but he could smell. There was a small brown cloud escaping from the metal box through a set of doors on the side that must have broken when it hit the ocean floor. Mako sniffed the cloud carefully. A strong scent filled his nose. It was like nothing he had ever smelled before in his life, and he had to eat whatever was making that smell!

The little shark squeezed through the doors and discovered a treasure of sweet-smelling cocoa beans. Mako couldn't help himself. He ended up eating every bean in that giant container. Bad idea.

As soon as Mako chomped down on the cocoa beans, his eyes grew wide and his smile became wider. In a flash, Mako was over-charged and bounced around the metal box until he broke through one of the sides.

Mako's never going to sleep again, Hammerhead had thought, watching her friend swim about in bursts of energy.

Now Hammerhead barely dodged Mako as he shot past. But when Hammerhead darted out of the way, she swam right into a coral reef. Her head slipped between the colorful corals, and when she tried to pull it back out, the broad blades of her head were stuck!

Hammerhead felt her cheeks turn red. At least Tiger Shark wasn't around to see her.

But then more fish from the reef swam out to see what was going on. They all erupted in bubbles of laughter at the silly shark.

Hammerhead's tail hung low. Why did the most embarrassing things always happen to her? She tried to lurch forward and scare the fish away, but it was useless. The coral wouldn't budge.

Then the fish stopped laughing. Hammerhead looked up to see Porbeagle swoop in and chase the fish right into the reef. After he was sure all the fish were gone, Porbeagle returned and helped free Hammerhead.

Hammerhead smiled and rubbed Porbeagle on the head. She knew that no matter what, Porbeagle would stick by her.

Mako swam back to them too. He had heard the commotion and wanted in on the action.

Even though Hammerhead knew it might not be a good idea to invite Mako to Tiburon Cove, she waved for the wild shark to follow them. And when she did, the three friends were already on their way.

The three friends were part of what Hammerhead liked to call the Terrestrial Science Club. Although she was pretty sure that she was the only shark interested in it, the three had banded together in a way she couldn't have with the other sharks in the ocean. They helped her on her quest and at least always *pretended* to be interested in terrestrial things.

In the cove, Hammerhead could relax while she studied the things that lived above the water. It was a strange world up there, and sharks were always discovering new types of creatures. Just the other day, Hammerhead had seen a "seagull." She heard a human call it a seagull; that was how she learned its name. Before that, she just called them *nee-yiy-yiy-yiy*s, because that was what they were always screeching, and wouldn't you expect them to be named whatever they screeched?

Hammerhead often wondered what a nee-yiy-yiy-yiy—no, wait, what a *seagull* tasted like. If she ate one, would it give her the power to fly? A flying shark would be cool. Hey, maybe then Tiger wouldn't pick on her! Because, you know, she could fly over and bite Tiger on the nose. Not that Hammerhead had ever thought of that, of course . . .

As the three sharks entered the cove, Hammerhead could smell something fleshy out on the beach. It smelled like humans.

You have got to be kidding, Hammerhead thought. After all *that*, was she still not going to get to go to the cove because the humans would scream in terror at the sight of them? What a day!

Normally, Hammerhead would retreat if she saw humans, but this time she just didn't care. She needed that land suit finished, and she needed it done quickly. She wanted to be cooler than Tiger!

But as Hammerhead got nearer, she realized the humans at the beach were an odd assortment. There were three of them, for one—there were never *three* people down at the cove. (Hammerhead often heard them remarking that it was a very, er, smelly place to be.) And they weren't bathing in the water or splashing one another or being rowdy. No, they looked interested in the tide pools. Hammerhead had never seen anyone like that before.

And if they're interested in the tide pools, she thought, *maybe they'd be interested in helping me find a new piece for my land suit.*

So Hammerhead did something that surprised even her. She stuck her fin out of the water and swam toward the shore.

FIVE

Wave Hello

N o way," said Kyle. "Uh-uh, not in a million years, you couldn't pay me enough money to go in the ocean around sharks."

Tammy rolled her eyes. "No one is going in the ocean, Kyle. We're just studying them. You know, for science."

"Come on, Kyle," Alex pleaded. "I've *never* been this close to a shark before. Just imagine the kind of art you can draw when you're that up close! Not only do the fins keep sharks steady when they swim, but they also let you know when a shark arrives at the party. It's all like, *Yo! Sharks in the house!*"

Now both Tammy and Kyle rolled their eyes.

"Listen, we are the Marine Science Club," Tammy started.

"Or MSC," interrupted Alex.

"Or the MSC," Tammy repeat-grumbled slowly. "So if anyone was going to use this opportunity to learn about and photograph some sharks, it's us."

The sharks floated in the water. It was as if they were waiting to see what the kids would do.

Even Kyle had to admit it. He felt drawn to these strange creatures.

"All right, I'm in," Kyle said. "What do we do now?"

Tammy jumped up from the tide pool. "First, let's split up. Kyle, you stay here. Alex, walk over to the left side of the cove, and I'll head to the right side. Maybe we'll be able to tell what kinds of sharks they are."

The kids split up. Tammy kept her eyes on the sharks as she walked. One floated along with her. When it came close to the surface, Tammy could immediately make out the odd flat shape of its face.

"Hammerhead," she muttered, then said it louder. "One of the sharks is a hammerhead!"

Alex's heart was beating hard in his chest, but it was the good kind of intense heartbeat. Like the one he got before his mom set out his favorite Sicilian pizza slice, with mushrooms and green bell peppers on top.

Alex could see one of the sharks traveling like an underwater cheetah beneath the cove. He knew there weren't many sharks who could move that quickly, and even fewer who could sustain themselves in this kind of water. Plus, this one was too small to be a great white shark. It was even too small to be a nurse shark. Alex was playing process of elimination, trying to determine which kind of shark it was . . .

Then a seagull dipped down to the water.

"Big mistake," Alex whispered.

Suddenly, the shark sprang out of the ocean and chomped madly in the air. The shark missed the bird, but it gave itself away. That nose, those snaggletoothed snappers, its precise motion and appetite . . . Alex smiled.

"This one is a mako shark," he cheered.

Kyle stared at the last shark who circled the middle of the cove. He watched as the shark flipped in circles, dragging a long tongue behind it.

"I think this one is broken," he told the others. "But I like it the best. It does tricks."

Tammy came running back. "Tricks? What do you mean?"

"Like doing flips, swimming in circles, and even floating upside down." Kyle pointed to the ocean and the shark became stiff, as if it were pointing back at him.

"Whoa," called out Alex from the other side of the beach. "I think it's *mimicking* you! Kyle, quick! Try something else!"

Kyle jumped up in the air and waved his hands. The shark disappeared deeper into the water.

"So much for that idea," said Kyle. "I must have scared it."

"No, wait!" called Tammy. "Look!"

There was a loud splash as Kyle's shark broke the surface of the water and shot into the air. It wiggled all its fins and tail and stuck out its tongue at the kids before crashing into the water.

Tammy jumped up and down too, smacking Kyle on the back. "That's a porbeagle! And it *is* totally mimicking you! We need to record this—no one is gonna believe this."

Tammy booted up the camera on her phone. But from this side of the cove, the location was too dark. She could see only a faint green glare on the bottom right of her screen.

Tammy sighed. A faint green glare wasn't going to be worth anything to them. Not front-page newspaper material, anyway. Not even a social media post.

Kyle could tell that Tammy was about to lose it, so he waved her over. "Forget the cameras for a second. Let's see what else these sharks can do."

SIX

Seashell Surfer

Hammerhead zipped back to Porbeagle's side. *Silly shark!* she thought. *You're going to scare the kids away by leaping out of the water and baring your teeth!*

In the long history between sharks and humans, one thing had always been true. Humans pretended to be big shark fans. They had a whole Shark Week and everything.

But when it came to real life . . . well, humans weren't the biggest fans of sharks there.

But the kids on this beach loved them. They kept jumping up and down off the sand dunes, and Porbeagle kept jumping out of the ocean. Hammerhead couldn't believe what she was seeing!

Then the kid with a mop of hair actually did a backflip! Not to be outdone, Mako rocketed out of the water and turned a triple sharkersault, which was when a shark flipped nose over tail and landed with a massive belly flop.

The kids cheered as the splash from Mako's trick rained down on the beach.

One of the kids held up a round yellow object and whistled. He bounced the object on the hard sand and it darted back up to his hand. Then he threw it toward them.

Oh no! It was all a trap! thought Hammerhead. *This was too good to be true. The humans must have thrown some sort of shark repellent device at us!*

Hammerhead ducked and waited for an explosion or an electric net to cover her, but the yellow object simply plopped in the water and floated above them. Hammerhead was not going to go near that thing.

Porbeagle, on the other hand, had to have it now! The shark wagged his tail and swam up like a torpedo, snagging the yellow object in his mouth. It was furry and wet and super chewy. While he was in the air, he saw the kids waving their arms. They must want this fuzzy, chewy thing back. So Porbeagle spit it out and smacked it with his tail.

The round thing flew through the air to the kids, who caught it. Then they all screamed with excitement.

Hammerhead wished she could make the kids cheer like that. Their laughter brought a smile to her face and it felt amazing. She circled the ocean floor, trying to think of what she could do to impress the humans.

Porbeagle swam up to his friend and nudged her forward.

Stop it, thought Hammerhead. *I'm concentrating over here!*

But Porbeagle wouldn't leave her alone. The small shark zipped all around her until she nearly scraped her fins on the colorful shells on the ocean floor.

Hey, shells! thought Hammerhead. *I could*

build the kids something from these!

Porbeagle nodded wildly and helped collect shells for Hammerhead. Mako helped too. Hammerhead worked in a creative fever. The water around her bubbled with the frantic imagination of a true shark artist at work. Mako and Porbeagle looked on as the dazzling display of shells formed into something new. Never before had Hammerhead's fins moved with such certainty. It was as if the sculpture were making itself.

When they finished, the three sharks moved back to admire the creation. Mako's jaw dropped and Porbeagle spun around in circles, though that was because he was chasing the pesky tail that was always following him!

I call it Surfer Dude, thought Hammerhead. It was perfect!

•

Well, with the hermit crab photo and my shark notes, I'm sure we'll still make the front page. Or maybe not the front page. Like, a medium page. But that's okay. That's progress! Tammy thought as she scribbled down notes about the sharks.

The sharks had followed the kids wherever they ran on the beach. They had jumped out of the water whenever the kids jumped off the dunes. The mako shark even did a loop the loop flip that looked like a circus act! And then Kyle threw a tennis ball at the sharks . . . and the porbeagle threw it back to them not once, not twice, but so many times that Kyle's arm got tired!

Kyle sketched the sharks in his notebook. As the three kids kept saying over and over, they didn't look like regular sharks. Sure, they looked familiar, but there was something special about them. Each one almost had its own personality.

Tammy had to admit, they actually kind of reminded her of the MSC members! The hammerhead shark was careful and a little head-strung about things, like Tammy. The porbeagle shark was friends with everyone, like Kyle. And the mako shark was a free spirit, like Alex.

I think we were meant to meet these sharks, Tammy thought. Almost like . . . she wasn't sure what, but it felt as if it were fate.

Then she heard lots of splashing.

The sharks were waving their tails above

the water to get the kids' attention. Tammy, Kyle, and Alex waded into the water, though only up to their ankles. The water was warm from the sun.

Tammy could tell this was the sharks' way of saying good-bye.

"Wait!" she called. "I have something for you." She waved rapidly, trying to get the sharks' attention.

Tammy had had the best day getting to know these sharks. It was the best she could remember—since she hung out with her grandfather in Japan, of course. The last Best Day Ever that Tammy had was when her grandfather gifted her the purple biodegradable hair ribbon.

"Use it well, *ojo*," Tammy's grandfather had said, calling her *princess* in Japanese.

Tammy loved the purple ribbon. But she realized now that it would be a good thank-you gift, from her to the sharks.

"Over here!" she hollered. "I have something for you!" Quickly, Tammy unwound the ribbon from her hair and dangled it above the water.

The porbeagle and the mako seemed suspicious, but the hammerhead swam eagerly up to her.

"It's biodegradable, meaning it won't last long and it won't hurt you, but it's special to me," Tammy said. "And I hope it's special to you. Thanks for meeting us."

The hammerhead opened its mouth wide. Tammy was scared, but she placed the ribbon gently on one of the hammerhead's teeth. The menacing shark seemed to nod, then disappeared underneath the water.

Suddenly, all the sharks' tails disappeared. Tammy blinked back tears. She knew their friends were gone.

But just as suddenly as they were gone, a new figure rose up from the ocean! It was a statue in the shape of a surfer made of shimmering seashells. And it was riding on a seashell surfboard! The statue caught a wave and rushed inland toward the kids. Tammy couldn't believe her own eyes. Had the sharks made this sculpture *for them*?

The sculpture was too big to take home, but Tammy snapped a photo anyway—of the sharks, the sculpture, everything. Maybe it wouldn't come out, but if she played with the settings just right on her computer, maybe it would.

Alex waded out farther and caught the seashell surfer sculpture. It was held together with mud from the bottom of the ocean and some trash that must have been down there too.

As Alex guided it back to the others, Tammy spied the hammerhead shark popping up its head. She locked eyes with it and smiled. Then she gave it a polite wave, as if to say, *Thank you.*

The hammerhead shark seemed to give her a wink. Then it, along with the other two sharks, dove back into the water and swam away.

Tammy couldn't believe it. Once the kids at school heard about this, they'd be begging her to join the MSC. She clutched her phone to her chest.

"I have to go home and edit this photo *right away*," she said.

"Right away?" Alex repeated. "You don't even want to come for pizza at my parents' place? They'd really like to meet—"

But before Alex could say anything else, Tammy was already zipping away and calling her mom to pick her up. She just hoped that the photo would come out okay, no matter what else happened.

SEVEN

Are You Afraid of the Shark?

Tammy sent the photo from her phone to her email address. Then she opened it up on a photo-editing system on her computer.

Admittedly, Tammy wasn't the *best* at graphic design or at photo editing, but she had done some light editing in the past on selfies and whatnot, so she hoped that would be enough to work. Besides, she *had* captured a bit of the hammerhead and the sculpture in this photo, if she closed one eye and poked her tongue out to see. Now it was time to spruce things up!

First, Tammy adjusted the brightness all the way to 100 percent. Then she used the sliders to scale it back down. She took out some contrast in the photo, which was apparently what made it dark. Then she turned it back up again.

Tammy played around for what must have been an hour. Filter, unfilter, slide, unslide. But by the time she was done, she could make out only a vague little outline of a shark.

"This is hopeless," she sighed. "It's never going to work."

But Tammy was determined to try anyway.

Submit to the Waverly Middle School Newspaper!

Have breaking news? Email or text Beckah Cohen today! We want to feature you!

She fished around in her school documents for information on submitting to the school newspaper.

Tammy stared at the leaflet in her hands. Of course, out of everyone in the school, the editor in chief of the newspaper *had* to be Beckah Cohen.

Tammy and Beckah had once been best friends. They'd lived on the same block, actually. It was the three of them, the Three Amigos: Tammy, Kyle, and Beckah. Then Beckah's family moved to the nicer part of town, and Tammy stopped hanging out with her so much. Beckah had wished Tammy a small "happy birthday" on that day, though, so maybe not all hope was lost.

Tammy took out her phone and searched Beckah's contact information. She had to admit, she was a little sad to see the two microphone emojis next to Beckah's name. Long before she'd been editor in chief, Beckah had wanted to be a singer. Now the emojis were just a sad reminder of what once was— now that Beckah was too cool for them, anyway.

Tammy dialed the number and waited while the phone rang.

"Hello?" came a voice. "This is Beckah."

"Becks," Tammy breathed. "It's Tammy. Hi."

And like any two friends who haven't really spoken in a while, the girls both braced themselves, wondering what was about to transpire.

"I saw that you're editor of the school newspaper. Congrats, Becks, that's really great," Tammy said, not sure what else to say.

"Thank you, Tammy," Beckah said. "And congratulations to you as well. Mr. Lopez said you're heading up some science club, right?"

"Marine science," Tammy replied. "The Marine Science Club, actually."

"Yes, yes, that was it. Well, that's very wonderful for you," Beckah replied.

"Actually I was calling you about the MSC. I was thinking maybe we could be featured in the paper. You can interview me, of course, and Kyle, obviously. And our third member, Alex!"

Tammy could hear Beckah bristle on the other end of the line.

"Er, Tammy," she said. "I don't mean to offend you, but you do know that we report *news*, right? I'm not so sure the Marine Science Club has done anything *newsworthy*."

"But that's where you're wrong!" Tammy snapped back. "We were just at the beach, and we went to Tiburon Cove, and—"

"Tiburon Cove?" Beckah repeated. "Tammy, you can't be serious. That place is awful, and it smells!"

"Yes, yes, Kyle already gave me that speech," Tammy replied. "But, Becks, listen, we went there, and we saw three—brace yourself—three *sharks*! Swimming out to us! They made us a gift—a sculpture! And we studied them, Beckah, with our own two eyes. Well, six eyes. Since there were three of us, but you know what I mean!"

Beckah sighed on the other end of the line. "Tammy," she said slowly, "do you have any *evidence* you saw these sharks?"

"Well, kind of, but—"

"*Kind of* and *evidence* aren't the same thing, Tammy," Beckah replied. Then her voice softened. "Look, I want to help you, I really do. I know how much this kind of stuff means to you. But if I print anything in the paper that isn't cold hard fact, my butt is on the line. You have to understand that, right?"

Now it was Tammy's turn to sigh. "I understand," she said.

"But I'll make you a deal, since we're old friends. You get me a nice, clear, crisp photo of these sharks, and I'll help you make your club the coolest club in the whole entire school. You have my word."

Tammy nodded, even though she knew Beckah couldn't see her. "Thanks, Becks," Tammy said. "That means a lot."

There was a silence on the phone, and

Tammy knew she had to break it.

"I miss you, you know," she said. "Kyle misses you. Our part of Waverly misses you. You're welcome to come to a Marine Science Club meeting anytime. We don't have a treasurer."

Beckah smiled, even though she knew Tammy couldn't see her, either.

"We'll see," she said, and then she hung up.

EIGHT
Something Smells Fishy

The Marine Science Club decided to meet back at Tiburon Cove on Monday after school.

Tammy was prepared now. She packed her backpack with water bottles for the three of them; her phone; an extra phone battery, just in case; and an old flashlight she'd found in her mom's drawer. If the sharks were out again, maybe Tammy could get a better photo, this time with the flashlight!

As Tammy and Kyle arrived at the boardwalk, there was already a floppy-haired kid waving back to them. He smiled a toothy grin.

"MSC meeting number *three*," Alex called out. "And good timing too. It's about to be low tide."

Tammy checked the tide clock app on her phone. Alex was right—the ocean was moving from high tide to low tide. The three friends made their way from the boardwalk to the outskirts of Tiburon Cove. They noticed that as the shoreline moved farther out, more tide pools were revealed.

On Saturday, when they saw the sharks, high tide had been coming in. Tammy worried that the sharks might have come and gone already. Maybe they missed them?

Kyle could read the look on Tammy's face. "They'll be here. Don't worry."

After a moment of sitting and watching, Alex said, "Hey, Tammy? I know you really want to get MSC into the school paper. But I wouldn't have believed me either if I hadn't seen what those sharks could do. So I brought a video camera this time. Maybe we can capture their movement and get on the *morning announcements*!"

Tammy looked up at Alex with a big, bright smile. She hadn't even thought of that! The morning announcements were broadcast to the whole school. It was maybe even a little cooler than the school newspaper!

"That's a great idea," Tammy said, beaming at her friend. "Now we just have to sit and wait."

And wait.

And wait.

And wait.

•

Hammerhead couldn't believe it. She kept turning the purple ribbon in her fins over and over.

Sure, it wasn't exactly a glass bowl, perfect for her land suit. But it was *something*! Even if that girl had said it would disintegrate.

Hammerhead was so interested in the ribbon, she hardly noticed a knocking at her sunken ship door until it got really, REALLY loud.

That knocking was coming from Mako. And he wasn't rapping on the wall politely with his fin like a normal shark. He was headbutting the wall, over and over and over and over!

Hammerhead waved for him to stop, but Mako wouldn't. His eyes were wider than usual, and he pointed to the ocean floor with his nose.

It's gotta be something important, Hammerhead realized, so she swam over to find out.

When Hammerhead reached Mako, she noticed a drawing in the sand that looked like a map of Tiburon Cove, with three stick-figure people on the beach and a drawing of a small shark with a long tongue in the water.

Oh, shark boy, thought Hammerhead. *The*

kids last time were nice, but this could be an entirely different set of folks! And poor unsuspecting Porbeagle went back to the beach without us! We have to go too!

In a flash of bubbles, Hammerhead and Mako thrust forward, hoping to join their curious and trusting friend. They swam as quickly as they could.

When they reached the water just on the outskirts of the cove, Hammerhead splashed around in a hurry. Porbeagle was nowhere to be found. *What happened to him?*

Mako pointed his fin at the three people, as if to say, *Look over there.*

Hammerhead turned toward them. She could almost breathe a sigh of relief! They *were* the same kids as before—she recognized the girl who had given her the prized ribbon.

But where was Porbeagle?

Mako rushed around frantically, looking behind sea rocks and algae clumps. He popped back up with a mess of kelp on his head that looked like the one human's floppy hair. Mako shook his muck-green mop as if to say, *I can't find him anywhere!*

Hammerhead was alarmed. Porbeagle was missing! This was an emergency, and emergencies called for extreme moves.

Hammerhead poked her head up above the water.

NINE
Poor Porbeagle

Kyle was the first one to notice the fins peeking out of the sea. "Look, the sharks are back!"

Tammy and Alex raced deeper into the water than they had last time. Kyle stayed behind, but the three friends could still hear one another.

Alex held up his camera, then waved to the sharks and yelled, "Hey! Over here! Do one of your amazing tricks, please? We'll make you famous! The biggest superstars of the ocean!"

"Wait," said Tammy. "Something's different this time. There are only two sharks, and they're swimming all over the place. Last time they were more—I don't know—more focused. Today, though . . ."

"Today they seem worried," Alex finished her thought.

"They don't seem worried to me," Kyle squealed as a crest of water shot toward them.

The water was coming from the hammerhead. Then as quickly as it swam, the shark stopped.

"It's stuck," said Tammy, looking over at Kyle and Alex. "It needs our help!"

"Wait, Tammy!" yelled Kyle, but it was too late.

The hammerhead shark was beached on a sandbar. Most of its body was still underwater, but its violet-blue back jutted out in the sun. Tammy didn't think twice. She moved through the ocean as the waves rolled gently past her.

Normally Tammy would *never* have done this. She would never approach a beached shark, especially not without parent supervision. But this was different. She could feel this was different.

Tammy reached out and touched the shark's back, making sure to stay far away from its jaws. The hammerhead's eye closest to Tammy softened as if the shark needed her. She felt the animal's ragged breath and immediately wanted to calm it down. She could sense that something was wrong.

"It's okay. You're going to be just fine," Tammy said, as if she were talking to a lost puppy.

But the shark kept wiggling. *Huh*, Tammy thought. Then she realized! The shark wasn't stuck at all.

"Guys," Tammy said, beckoning her friends. "I think this shark stopped on its own, almost like it wanted to get our attention."

And just when Tammy said that, the mako shark leaped into the air. It stuck its tongue out at Kyle, just as the porbeagle had done on Saturday.

To Tammy's surprise, Kyle was the first one to connect the dots. "Porbeagle," he said solemnly. "They're telling us that the porbeagle is in trouble!"

Tammy focused on the hammerhead shark.

"Porbeagle . . . is trapped?" she guessed. No response from the sharks. "Porbeagle . . . is missing?"

As she said that, the hammerhead shark twisted around and nodded wildly, splashing its T-shaped head in and out of the water.

"That's it! The porbeagle shark is missing!" Tammy yelled to the others. "But how can a shark just go missing? We've got to help them find their friend!"

Alex fished a pair of binoculars out of his back pocket. He adjusted the knobs on them and scanned the ocean, but there was nothing that he could see.

"No splashes," Alex said sadly. "Nada."

Tammy's mind was racing. The sharks wanted their help. This might be a first-ever *real* human-shark interaction. Forget the

MSC being *cool*; this was downright momentous! She could feel herself panicking for the little porbeagle shark too.

Tammy sat back and thought. Where could the porbeagle have gone? It was low tide now . . . *low tide!*

Of course! If the porbeagle wasn't here in low tide, had it swum out earlier? During high tide?

"High tide!" said Tammy. "That must be it! If the porbeagle came to find us at high tide, it might have swum into the cave. But when the tide went out, it could have gotten trapped in a deep tide pool!"

Alex grabbed his video camera and ran quickly, but he accidentally dropped it along the way.

"Oh no," Alex sighed when he saw it crash

to the shore and make a *beep!* but there was nothing he could do about it.

Tammy and Kyle followed him until they were back by the tide pools. But whereas Kyle and Alex stayed inside, Tammy stuck her feet in the water.

A faint splashing sound echoed off the walls of Tiburon Cove.

It was Kyle, with his incredible artist's brain, who located the sound and pointed to a tide pool farther back in the cave. "There!" he said.

Tammy took off her backpack and put it on the ground. She grabbed her flashlight and switched it on. Although she'd originally wanted to photograph the sharks, that didn't matter anymore. All she cared about was saving the porbeagle. She couldn't think of anything else!

The sound became louder and louder. Tammy tried to stand, but her ankle got trapped in some seaweed. She needed to untangle herself!

While Tammy worked on untying herself, Kyle moved closer to the noise.

"It's the porbeagle!" Kyle gasped, edging closer to it and farther from Tammy.

The poor porbeagle shark was trapped in a tide pool. Normally, the porbeagle shark could have gotten out, but similar to Tammy, the creature was tangled in a plastic six-pack yoke.

Alex looked at the shark, and his heart suddenly felt very heavy. "It's completely trapped," he said sadly.

TEN
Shark Out of Water

Whoa, easy, boy," Kyle told the shark. "We're here to help."

The porbeagle shark was still very alarmed, trying its best to get out of the tide pool.

"Of course it doesn't trust us," Alex said. "Humans are the ones who invented those plastic things, remember? *And* the ones who probably didn't dispose of it properly, making him get caught."

But the porbeagle still wouldn't relent.

Finally, Tammy untied herself. She was free! She turned to the hammerhead shark, who had arrived right by the ledge where she'd stuck in her feet.

"We want to *help*," Tammy said slowly, emphasizing the word "help." "Can you tell your friend?"

Hammerhead seemed to nod. Then it emitted a great big bubble.

Tammy wasn't sure if the bubble meant anything, but then again, she didn't speak Shark. It clearly meant something to the porbeagle, because the little shark instantly relaxed. It looked at Kyle with hope in its eyes.

"I'm going to be honest," Kyle said as Tammy got closer. "I don't think I'm qualified enough to handle this. I wouldn't even be here if it weren't for you guys. Tammy, you should do it. You're the president of the MSC."

Tammy nearly laughed. "President of the MSC? Kyle, forget the MSC!" she said. "This isn't about some dumb Waverly Middle School club; this is about doing *real stuff*. And I *know* you can do this, Kyle. I know you weren't really interested in marine science at first, but you've learned so much. Who cares if we're not the coolest club in school? *We* think we're the coolest, and so long as we think we are, that's all that matters."

Alex smiled at Kyle. "You got this, buddy," he said.

The hammerhead and the mako seemed to agree.

Carefully, Kyle eased his hand into the

water. He watched as the little porbeagle relaxed. Kyle gently touched the porbeagle's tail and tried to slide off the plastic ring, but it was too tight.

"I can't do this," Kyle said again, looking defeated.

"You *have* to do this," Tammy told him.

"We believe in you," said Alex.

With his friends' words close to his heart, Kyle tried again. He slipped his nail into the plastic and tugged at it with all his might. Then Kyle let out a *gasp*! The porbeagle shark was free!

The porbeagle let out a huge bubble, and the other sharks jumped for joy. Tammy and Alex screeched, *"Wahoo! Kyle, you did it!"*

Kyle smiled to himself. "Huh," he said, "I guess I did it."

Then the porbeagle gave Kyle's arm a soft nuzzle with its nose.

"I think it likes you," said Alex. Then, with Tammy's flashlight still illuminating everything, he was finally able to look around the dark cave. "Look at this mess! People don't realize what kind of damage we're doing to our oceans and beaches."

"Yeah, but the sharks do," said Kyle as he patted the porbeagle's back. The small shark swam back and forth under his grasp, like a puppy dog searching for a scratch behind the ear.

"Maybe people just need to see what's going on and they'd help make a difference," suggested Alex. "My parents buy soda on those six-pack plastic rings all the time for their pizza shop. They don't mean to cause harm, but this could very easily have been from their new shop." Alex looked really sad.

"You can't beat yourself up over that," Tammy said. "Besides, if you cut those pieces of plastic into bits, you can make sure the animals won't get stuck in them, just in case it ends up in the ocean."

That gave Kyle an idea. "What if we organized a beach cleanup?" he said. "I know MSC isn't exactly cool, but if we got the teachers on board and organized it as a field trip during the day, I think lots of Waverly Middle School kids would be interested. And it would stop the trash from harming the sharks."

Tammy and Alex smiled. "Kyle, that's brilliant," Alex said.

The sharks splashed some more, and

Tammy realized this was probably them saying good-bye again.

"I hope to see you all soon," Tammy told the sharks. "We'll come back. I promise."

The sharks splashed again, as if thanking her. Then the hammerhead shark brought a purple shell up to the surface. Tammy knew it was thanking them not only for saving the porbeagle, but also for the gift she'd given it, since the shell was purple, like her ribbon.

Tammy, Alex, and Kyle collected everything they'd dropped behind and walked away. Even though they had no way to prove it, they knew that this wasn't the last time they'd see their shark friends.

ELEVEN
Keep It Clean

Tammy had to admit it: Alex's parents' pizza was *delicious*.

"So I was thinking about your biodegradable hair ribbon, and I think we can incorporate some biodegradable plates and utensils into the restaurant," Alex said. "I'll talk to my parents about it later, but I think they'd really like that plan."

"That's awesome," said Kyle. "Almost as

awesome as this *pizza*!" He dug in to his slice. Opened up next to him was his sketchbook. Kyle was drawing the porbeagle eating pizza.

"I'm just sorry we didn't get any kind of footage or photography for the MSC. That would've really been amazing," Alex told Tammy. He picked up the video camera he'd dropped while running.

"It's a bummer, but it's okay," Tammy said. "Like I said, helping marine life is way more important than being cool."

Then Tammy furrowed her brow. "Hey, what's that?" she asked, pointing to a faint red light flashing on the video camera.

"Huh, I guess it's recording," Alex said. "I didn't press record, though. I don't know why—"

Tammy nearly spit out her delicious extra-cheesy pizza. "Alex, I think when you dropped it, the camera accidentally turned on and started recording! Play it back, play it back!"

Alex did as instructed. Kyle stuck his face in to see too. And sure enough, the camera had recorded not just their pizza get-together but the whole rescue of the porbeagle too!

"Dudes!" Alex nearly shouted. "This—this means . . ."

"Our beach cleanup is about to get a whole *lot* bigger," Kyle said.

Tammy couldn't help it. She smiled from ear to ear.

"The Marine Science Club is on the *map*, baby," she said. "I'll give the Waverly Middle School paper a call tonight—this is grade A news they will *not* want to miss. Hey, maybe I'll even contact the local news. This is going to be the biggest, baddest ocean cleanup there's ever been. And it's all thanks to you guys. Seriously, thank you both. I couldn't ask for two better founding members of the MSC."

Kyle smiled. "I was thinking about that, actually," he said. "And if you're president, Tammy, and you're VP, Alex—maybe it *is* a good idea that I become treasurer."

Tammy couldn't help herself. She whooped, and whooped loud.

"Would you really be our treasurer?" she asked, smiling at her friend. "Oh, Kyle!" She scooped him up in a big hug, then and there.

"Hey, I think this is cause for some

celebration," Alex said. He stuck his fist into the middle of the table and stared up at the other two hopefully.

Tammy and Kyle exchanged a hesitant look. Then they laughed and stuck their fists in too.

"Science!" they all said together.

Although Tammy, Kyle, and Alex were safe, don't **ever** approach a wild shark! If you see one in the ocean, make sure you alert an adult.

Porbeagle Shark

Most porbeagle sharks live in the North Atlantic and the Southern Hemisphere. They like to swim in cold water. The porbeagle shark eats mostly bony fish. It has a highly active lifestyle.

Hammerhead Shark

Hammerhead sharks have wide eyes that set them apart! On average, they live twenty to thirty years and can weigh as much as 1,000 pounds. Stingrays are hammerheads' favorite meal, and the sharks use the stingray's unique shape to locate their prey.

Mako Shark

Mako sharks are found all over the world. They are one of the fastest sharks out there and weigh in at around 375 pounds. These sharks are known for jumping out of the water. Scientists believe this is how they search for their prey.